4

5

size (180 tablets), $1.00.

8

7

8

9

10

green
gra

Gabriel

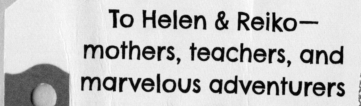

To Helen & Reiko—
mothers, teachers, and
marvelous adventurers

Henry Holt and Company, *Publishers since 1866*
Henry Holt® is a registered trademark of Macmillan Publishing Group, LLC
120 Broadway, New York, New York 10271 · mackids.com

Library of Congress Cataloging-in-Publication Data
Names: Alko, Selina, author. Title: One golden rule at school : a counting book / Selina Alko.
Description: First edition. | New York : Christy Ottaviano Books, Henry Holt and Company, 2020. |
Audience: Ages 2–6. | Audience: Grades K–1. |
Summary: Illustrations and simple, rhyming text reveal a day at school, from one backpack to seven stars
on a chart and back down again. Includes additional groups of objects that can be counted, up to twenty.
Identifiers: LCCN 2019039256 | ISBN 9781250163813 (hardcover)
Subjects: CYAC: Stories in rhyme. | Schools–Fiction. | Counting.
Classification: LCC PZ8.3.A4 One 2020 | DDC [E]–dc23
LC record available at https://lccn.loc.gov/2019039256

Our books may be purchased in bulk for promotional, educational, or business use.
Please contact your local bookseller or the Macmillan Corporate and Premium Sales Department at
(800) 221-7945 ext. 5442 or by email at MacmillanSpecialMarkets@macmillan.com.

First edition, 2020 / Design by Angela Jun and Vera Soki
Acrylics, watercolors, salt, pencils, and collage on Strathmore illustration board
were used to create the art for this book.
Printed in China by RR Donnelley Asia Printing Solutions Ltd., Dongguan City, Guangdong Province

1 3 5 7 9 10 8 6 4 2

CAT. No. 23-243   PRINTED IN U.S.

One Golden Rule at School

A Counting Book

Selina Alko

Christy Ottaviano Books
Henry Holt and Company
New York

Aa
apple

1 GLOBE

1 APPLE

PET
FISH

ADMIT
ONE

ONE backpack.

2 PENCILS

2 NOTEBOOKS

TWO teachers.

THREE posters on the wall.

FOUR stories.

5 FALL LEAVES

5 EGGS

NATURE

GOOD FOR 5 CENTS IN TRADE

FIVE small plants.

SIX blocks stacked up tall.

6
PAPER
AIRPLANES

SKY
SCRAPER
center

OPEN

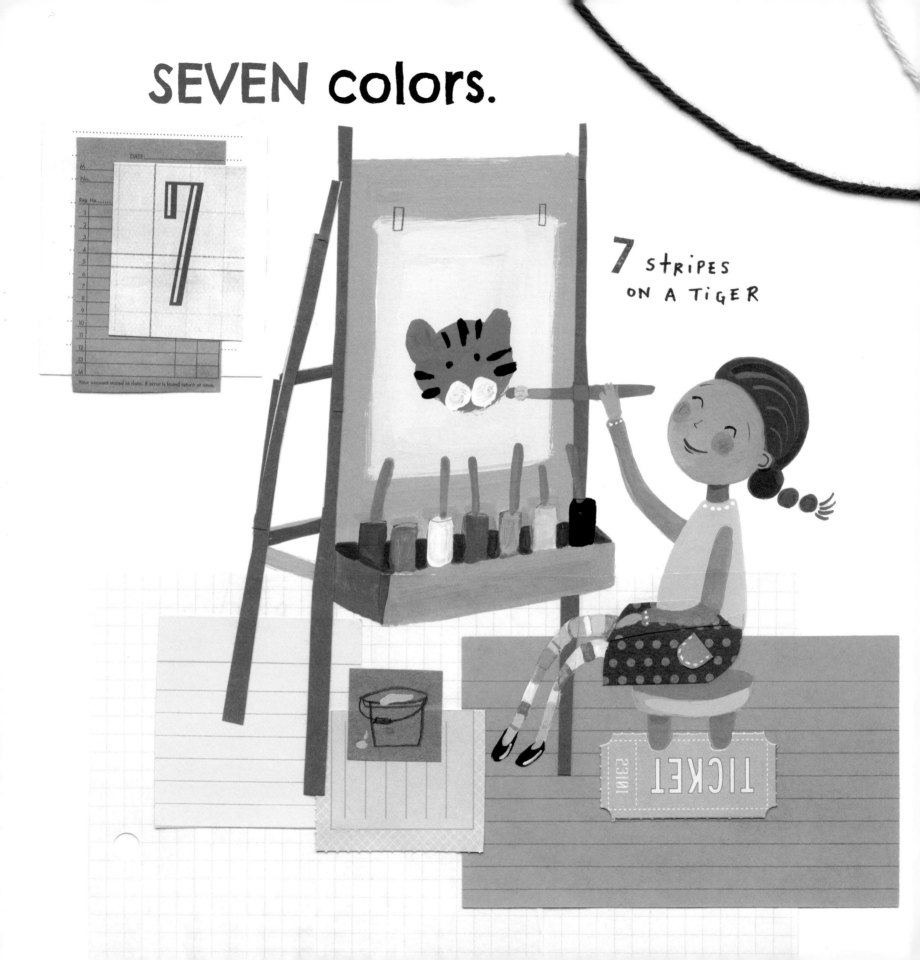

SEVEN colors.

7 STRIPES ON A TIGER

MUSIC

ART

8

8 NOTES

8 MUSICAL INSTRUMENTS

EIGHT letters.

May 30

THE GOLDEN RULE
DO to OTHERS as YOU WOULD
HAVE THEM DO to YOU

9

9 green grapes

NINE buttons click and chime.

TEN chickpeas line up,

all set for snack time.

NINE round balls.

8
STARS

8

EIGHT puppets.

SEVEN stars on the chart.

FIVE poses.

FOUR bins filled with art.

4

4 DRAWINGS

THREE quick claps.

TWO shoes on.

2 Books

2 PENCILS

ONE Golden Rule.

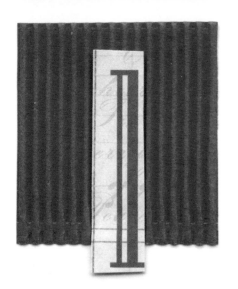

ONE backpack.

ONE zip up.

ONE great day at school!

How High Can You Count?

11

12 JAN FEB MAR APR MAY JUN JUL AUG

13

14

15

16

17

18

19

20

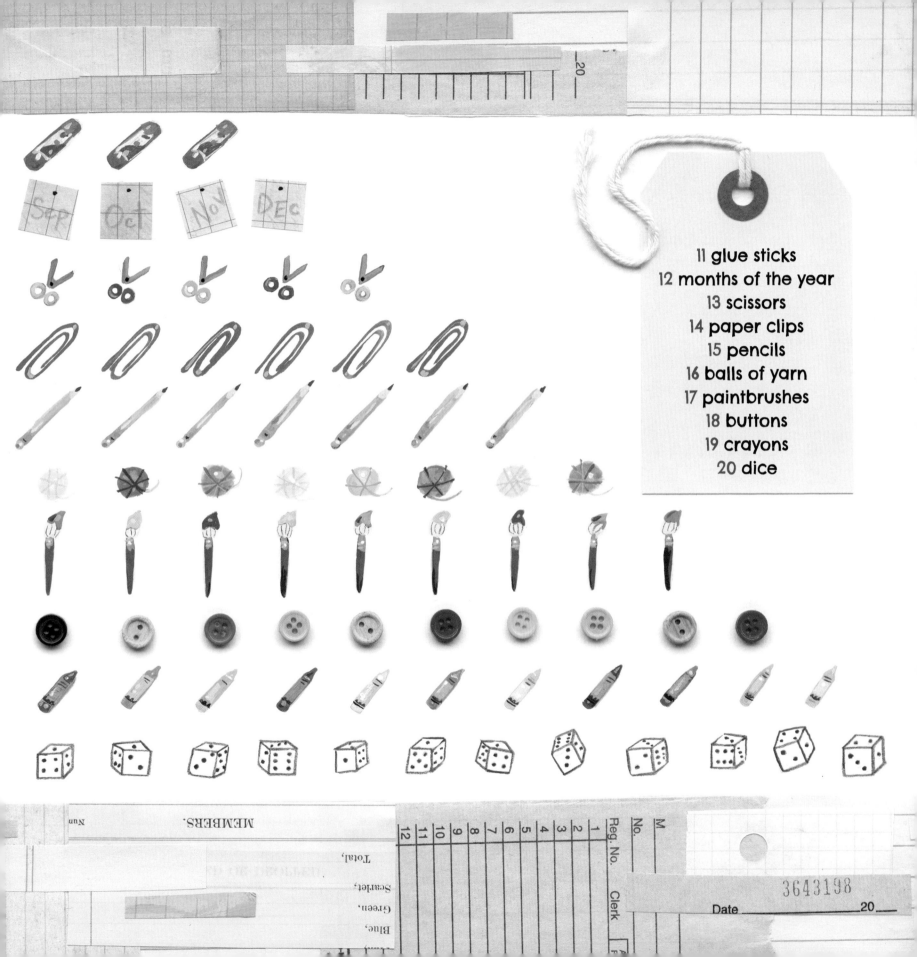

11 glue sticks
12 months of the year
13 scissors
14 paper clips
15 pencils
16 balls of yarn
17 paintbrushes
18 buttons
19 crayons
20 dice

10   9   8

5   4

BORROWER'S CARD

No.

Name